PIG-BOY

A TRICKSTER TALE FROM HAWAI'I

Gerald McDermott

Harcourt Children's Books

Houghton Mifflin Harcourt   New York   2009

Requests for permission to make copies of any part of the work should be submitted online at www.harcourt.com/contact or mailed to the following address: Permissions Department, Houghton Mifflin Harcourt Publishing Company, 6277 Sea Harbor Drive, Orlando, Florida 32887-6777.

Harcourt Children's Books is an imprint of Houghton Mifflin Harcourt Publishing Company.

www.hmhbooks.com

Library of Congress Cataloging-in-Publication Data
McDermott, Gerald.
Pig-Boy: a trickster tale from Hawai'i/by Gerald McDermott.
p. cm.
Summary: The mischievous, shape-shifting Pig-Boy gets in trouble with both the King and Pele, the goddess of fire, but always manages to slip away as his grandmother has told him to do.
[1. Folklore—Hawaii.] I. Title.
PZ8.1.M159Pig 2009
398.2—dc22   [E] 2006035426
ISBN 978-0-15-216590-1

First edition
H G F E D C B A

Printed in Singapore

The illustrations in this book were done in gouache, colored pencil, and pastel on 400 lb. Arches watercolor paper.
The text type was set in Cantoria MT Std.
The display lettering was created by Gerald McDermott.
Color separations by Bright Arts Ltd., Hong Kong
Printed and bound by Tien Wah Press, Singapore
Production supervision by Pascha Gerlinger
Designed by Lydia D'moch and Michele Wetherbee

Pig-Boy is drawn from the stories of Kamapua'a, a divine trickster-hero in Hawaiian mythology. Kamapua'a is a shape-shifter. In human form, he is a handsome warrior. In his pig form, he is a trickster who provokes the powerful.

Sometimes he is a wild piglet, sometimes a voracious hog, rooting in the dark, moist earth. Sometimes he's a monstrous boar with eight eyes and four tusks curled like the crescent moon. Ever changing, this mischief-maker is a lunar animal that can escape pursuers by transforming into the pig-nosed fish (*humu-humu-nuku-nuku-āpua'a*) or the *kukui* tree or the elegant *'ama'u* fern (singed red, it is said, by the fiery wrath of the goddess Pele).

Hawaiian mythology, the ancient tales that celebrate the many deities of the islands, was oral lore until the nineteenth century, when it began to be transcribed, most notably by G. W. Kahiolo in 1861. In 1891 the Kamapua'a epic was first published in *Ka Leo o ka Lahui*, a Hawaiian-language newspaper.

With *Pig-Boy*, as with all my books, I hope my version excites the imagination and provokes exploration of the vital mythological tradition from which it is drawn. The more one discovers about another's culture, the more deeply one may perceive our common humanity.

I'm grateful to Nyla Fujii-Babb for the rich insights that flow from her deep knowledge of Hawaiian tradition. I also thank Alice Mak for guiding me through the archives of the University of Hawai'i at Mānoa, Mora Ebie for her excellent and tireless research assistance, Robert Walter for his valuable suggestions and encouragement, and my editor Jeannette Larson for wrangling *Pig-Boy* to completion.

—G. M.

www.geraldmcdermott.com

For Leighton

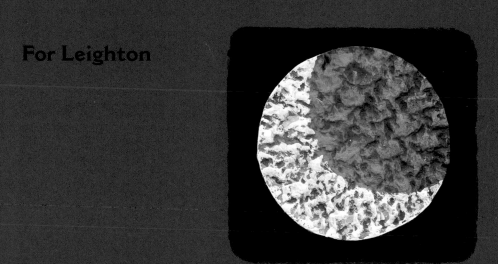

ig-Boy!

When he was born, he was a hairy little hog.
His ears were pointy and his tail was curly.
His back was bristly and his snout was dirty.

Grandmother loved this dirty little boy.
She wrapped him in soft leaves
and sang him to sleep.

"You will be a little pig who roots in the earth.
You will be a hairy hog who sails the seas.
You will be a tiny fish who swims in the ocean.
You will be a wild boar who carves the mountains.
You will be filled with magic.

And if trouble comes," she whispered, "just slip away."

When Pig-Boy awoke,
he was very hungry.
He began to eat.

As he ate, he began to burp.
As he burped, he ate more
and more and more.

Uurrrp! He had eaten all the roots in his grandmother's taro patch and he was *still* hungry.

Pig-Boy ran into the king's gardens and stole the royal chickens.

The king and his men chased after the greedy hog.
They found him in the middle of the forest.
"Seize him!" the king commanded.

Pig-Boy squealed and became
a hundred little piglets.

Then he slipped away.

Pig-Boy was rowing! Pig-Boy was sailing!
Pig-Boy was flying over the waves,
rushing toward Pele.

But when Pele saw the dirty,
hairy little hog, she shouted,
"Swine! Leave me alone!"
She shook the earth.
She filled the sky with fire
and smoke.

Pig-Boy squealed and jumped
into the ocean.

He became the pig-nosed fish called
humu-humu-nuku-nuku-āpua'a.
Then he slipped away.

When Pig-Boy leaped
out of the water, the king
was waiting.

Pig-Boy was caught!
The king's men tied him to a pole and carried him away.

Snort!

He grew bigger and bigger
and bigger until he burst free.

Grunt!

Pig-Boy ripped a path up the mountain with his bristly back.
The waters rushed down and washed away the king and his men.

Then Pig-Boy got small.
He ran to Grandmother.
She wrapped him in soft leaves
and sang him to sleep.

Pig-Boy is a dreamer.
He dreams of roaming the islands
and sailing the seas
and swimming the ocean
and climbing the mountains.

And if trouble comes,
as it always does,
he just slips away.